P9-CEX-362

FERGUS

THE FARMYARD DOG

DISCARD

FERGUS

The Farmyard Dog

Tony Maddox

The warm, sunny farmyard was a perfect place for Fergus to take a nap. But every-time he closed his eyes, he heard noises—quack, quack, quack of the ducks... cluck, cluck, cluck of hens... oink, oink, oink of pigs. How was Fergus ever going to get some sleep? Then, worst of all, there came a new noise: squeak, squeak, squeak! What was causing the mysterious squeak? Toddlers will love to imitate the animal sounds as they hear this story—and they'll love Tony Maddox's humorous illustrations too.

To Natalie, Zara, Chloe, Holly and Jamie

First edition for the United States, Canada,
and the Philippines published 1993 by
Barron's Educational Series, Inc.

First published 1992 by Piccadilly Press Ltd.,
London, England.

Text and illustration copyright © Tony Maddox, 1992

All inquiries should be addressed to:
Barron's Educational Series, Inc.
250 Wireless Boulevard
Hauppauge, New York 11788

International Standard Book No. 0-8120-6373-2 (H)
0-8120-1763-3 (PB)

Library of Congress Catalog Card No. 93-738

Library of Congress Cataloging-in-Publication Data
Available on request.

Tony Maddox is British and lives in Worcestershire with his wife. He illustrates
greetings cards as well as books. Barron's was the American publisher of
his first picture book, *Spike, The Sparrow Who Couldn't Sing!*

PRINTED IN BELGIUM
3456   9697   987654321

FERGUS
THE FARMYARD DOG

Peabody Public Library
Columbia City, IN

Tony Maddox

Barron's

Fergus the farmyard dog lay in the
warm sunshine and tried to sleep. But
all he could hear was the *Cluck,
Cluck, Cluck* of the hens in the yard.

And the *Quack, Quack, Quack* of the ducks by the pond.

Then he heard the *Squeak* . . . *Squeak* . . . *Squeak* of . . .
Fergus looked around.
What was making that noise?

The sheep in the meadow were going
Baa, Baa, Baa.

The pigs in their pen were going
Oink, Oink, Oink.
Squeak . . . Squeak . . . Squeak . . .
What could it be?

He ran to the barn.
The cows went
Moo, Moo, Moo.
Squeak . . . Squeak . . .
Squeak . . .
What's that noise?

He ran to the paddock. The donkey went *Hee Haw, Hee Haw!*

Fergus sat down, raised both ears and listened as hard as he could.

*Cluck, Cluck, Quack, Quack,
Squeak . . .*
There it was!
Baa, Baa, Oink, Oink, Squeak . . .
There it was again!
Moo, Moo, Hee Haw, Squeak!

It seemed to be coming from the
garden behind the farmhouse.
Squeak . . . Squeak . . . Squeak . . .
Fergus crept up and peeked through
the open gate to see . . .

. . . Farmer Bob asleep in
the old garden seat
that hung from
the apple tree.

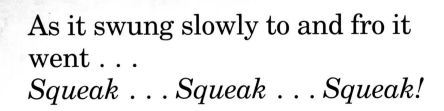

As it swung slowly to and fro it went . . .
Squeak . . . Squeak . . . Squeak!

"Woof, Woof!" went Fergus.
Farmer Bob woke up with a start.
"What's wrong, Fergus?" he said.
"Woof, Woof, Woof!" went Fergus again.

Then Farmer Bob noticed the squeak. "Is that what's wrong? he said. "I'll fix that! A bit of oil should do the trick."

When the squeaky parts had been oiled, Farmer Bob sat back on the seat and Fergus jumped up beside him.

BRRRRRR
BRRRRRRRR

OIL

In no time at all the two of them
were asleep.

Brrrrrrrrrrrrr. Brrrrrrrrrrrrr!

What's THAT noise?